The
Lucky
Ones

The
Lucky
Ones

FIVE JOURNEYS TOWARD A HOME

by Elizabeth Jane Coatsworth

illustrated by Janet Doyle

The Macmillan Company, New York

Collier-Macmillan Limited, London

The Macmillan Company, New York
Collier-Macmillan Canada, Ltd., Toronto, Ontario
Library of Congress catalog card number: 68–20612
Printed in the United States of America

FIRST PRINTING

To all those people who

in every part of the world

are working to make

new homes for the homeless

BUT WAS IT NEAR OR FAR?

From my world to your world, how far is it?
Surely not very far: a well-worn footpath,
A wall or two to climb, perhaps, and the beechwood
To go through; perhaps a stream to ford
By tipping stepping-stones; surely that is all,
Or is there more? That sudden vista now
Of half a world, or is it half a universe
Between us? And the roll of lonely seas
Without an island in them? Are there stars,
Galaxies of space, or only one small field
Between your world and mine? Listen! Listen!
Can you hear my voice? What's that? What's that?
It sounded like the wind, but was your voice,
Your voice, of course,
But was it near or far?

FOREWORD

In these stories, Elizabeth Coatsworth captures the poignancy of a world unseen by most of us but which has now become so real to so many refugee children.

They become refugees partly because they were born in the twentieth century—often called the "Century of the Homeless Man." They are refugees from wars, great and small—World War II, Vietnam, Algeria, Sudan, Rwanda. They are refugees from revolutions, social, political, tribal, religious as in Africa and Asia. Most of them, especially the children, are the innocent victims of hatred and fighting, in which they do not share, and which they do not understand. They have fled because they have lost their homes, and for fear of their lives, and they are seeking new homes and peace—peace of heart and hearth. They find peace and a new life —bit by tiny bit, as these stories say.

All these stories are "true" as anyone can see and feel who ever saw a refugee camp. Time and place are not very important. The Algerian war is over, and so is World War II in Europe, but the story of the refugee, running into the night hungry, homeless and alone, is still true, and the story of his lonely and gallant effort to make a new life for himself and his family—that too is true. These are called "The Lucky Ones" only because they are alive and safe. They would be really "lucky" if they could find a friend—if thousands of them could find friends who understood the stories and were willing to help.

R. NORRIS WILSON
Executive Vice President
United States Committee for Refugees

Contents

The Man
of the Family

THE KITE

If I had a kite
(They cost money to buy!)
It would carry a whistle
To sound in the sky—
If I had a kite.

If I had a kite
It would dance on its string
And the sea-wind would play
With my pretty plaything—
If I had a kite.

If I had a kite
The birds would all say,
"What bird is that flying
So high and so gay?"—
If I had a kite.

But I haven't a kite
(They cost money to buy!)
So I'll choose out the best
Of the kites I see fly,
And pretend that it's mine
Up there in the sky—
My kite in the sky.

The Man
of the Family

Chang Ping was the man of his family. He was ten years old. His father was dead, and he lived in Hong Kong with his mother, who was ill, and his little sister, Blue Lotus. Their home was a temporary one-room shack made of flattened oil tins in one of the refugee settlements built in and around the city, which at all times has a million refugees, and sometimes more.

The Chang family did not have much to eat and not even much to drink. Every fourth day, Ping waited in a long, long line of other refugees to fill a heavy oil tin with water, which he carried carefully, using all his strength, up the hill to the shack.

This was drinking water, cooking water, bathing water and laundry water for all the family. The Changs were very careful of it, but somehow they and all the things about them managed to be clean.

One early morning, before it was time to go down to the market to sell the vegetables which a cousin raised outside the city, they sat on the rocky ledge beside their hut.

"It is beautiful," said Mrs. Chang, looking down over the roofs below them to the great harbor with its mass of houseboats and sampans, its rocky islands and, beyond them all, the sharp shine of the open sea.

"There is a kite!" cried Ping suddenly.

Far below them, a kite was indeed mounting into the air, a green kite, with a beautiful long tail.

"I wish I had a kite," said Blue Lotus, who sometimes spoke without thinking.

Her mother smiled at her. "You may have that kite, Blue Lotus," she said. "It is yours and Ping's. See how bravely it rises! It is bucking against its string like a fine horse against its halter!"

"Now it is losing height," cried Ping. "Up! Up! Kite!"

"It is obeying you," cried Blue Lotus. "And see! There is another come to join our kite."

So they sat in the sun. The sun was good for Mrs. Chang, and the children loved it. Now the city below them began to waken, and the kites were drawn down from their high air, like unwilling hawks returning to their masters' wrists.

Mrs. Chang sighed. "It is time for us to meet our cousin in the marketplace," she said. "The day is so fine, there should be many people out to buy."

Ping brought two baskets hung on a wooden yoke, like empty scales. His mother quickly made sure that she had the market license with her.

"Off we go," said Mrs. Chang.

The cousin was an elderly man and very lame. He was a hard worker and a good farmer. Every day he brought in vegetables from the little plot of land which he worked. He was too busy to sit in the all-day market waiting for customers, and, then, he was glad to help his cousin, Mrs. Chang, and her children. Were they not of the same blood? Two-thirds of the money from the sales went to him, and one-third to her.

This morning as the Changs came into the market, they found a young man sitting in their usual place, with his wares spread out before him, pretending not to see them.

Ping was the man of the family.

"Get out!" he shouted, hurrying toward the stranger.

"It's my place as much as yours. Get out yourself!" answered the young man, not moving.

"Son of a pig!" cried Ping.

"Son of a squeaking sparrow!" shouted the young man.

At once people began to gather, attracted by the sound of loud voices. Wherever something is happening, the Hong Kong crowd gathers.

"The place is theirs," said an old woman who sold flowers near them.

"Of course it is," shouted a girl who sold fish just behind them.

"Someone should call the market superintendent," said a man holding a cage of live birds.

"Mind your own business, you apes!" shouted the young man, growing angrier and angrier.

"I shall throw stones at you," threatened Ping.

"And if the boy hurts you, we will tell the police that the fault was yours," shrieked the crowd, delighted by the excitement.

Suddenly the young man gave up. Too many people were against him. Sullenly he gathered his wares and made off, and Ping, amid the congratulations of the crowd, unfolded the clean cloths on top of the baskets, laid them on the ground, and spread out the vegetables in small piles.

Mrs. Chang sat down on the curb. The shouting frightened and tired her, but she had not interfered.

Ping was the man of the family. He must protect them when it was necessary.

"Do not be worried," said the old woman who had first spoken up for them, noticing Mrs. Chang's distress. "I know the fellow. He is like a crow, always trying to make off with something not his own. But like a crow, he is a coward. He flies away as soon as there is trouble."

Early in the afternoon, Mrs. Chang left the market to go to the foreign woman doctor for more medicine. She had never mentioned her illness, but some neighbor must have told the foreigners about her coughing, and the doctor had sent for her. After the first, Mrs. Chang had not been frightened. And she did carefully everything she was told to do.

This afternoon the foreign doctor was very pleased with her. "You are much better," she said, "and I have more good news. I have had a chance to put your name down for two rooms in one of the new apartment houses which the city is putting up."

"Oh," said Mrs. Chang. "Heaven is good, and you are good. Thank you."

"You seem happy," said Ping when she returned to the market.

"Yes, the foreign lady told me that I am better," said his mother. She did not speak of the promise of a little apartment. When one has nothing, it is better for the young not to build on hope, for fear of being disappointed. But for her, the thought was like a flower.

Now it was time for Ping to get his shoeshine box and go to work downtown, to earn a little more money, while his mother and Blue Lotus met the cousin and gave him his share of the market profits and returned the unsold vegetables. Afterward, climbing the steep path for home, they usually met Ping coming down with his shoeshine box.

But there was something that Mrs. Chang and Blue Lotus did not know. Ping had only one secret in his life, one thing which he hid from his family for fear that it would cause them sorrow. Still he could not get rid of this wish, which filled his heart and mind. Every day when he left the market to get his box, he ran as fast as he could—and he was a fast runner—not for home, but straight for the nearest government school. There he stood hidden, a little behind the gate, watching the children coming out. The boys were dressed in white shirts and dark blue shorts, with socks and shoes, not sandals like Ping's. Most of them carried school satchels, and to Ping these satchels seemed the most wonderful possessions in the world. The children

never noticed him. They had too many things to talk and laugh about to notice a boy watching them from behind the gate, his heart in his eyes.

After a minute, Ping would tear himself away and hurry off up the steep streets and along the steeper paths to the high-perched tin shack which was home. He reached it, panting, but by the time he met his mother with Blue Lotus, slowly climbing out of the city, he was calm and smiling.

This had gone on for a long time, and no one guessed Ping's secret, not even in the refugee village, where everyone knew everyone else's business.

But on the day when Ping drove off the young man who had tried to steal their place in the market, something new happened. Perhaps because Mrs. Chang felt happy, she decided to buy some needles on the way home. With the yoke and its empty market baskets on one shoulder and Blue Lotus beside her, she walked down a street of little shops, where she seldom went and which happened to pass the school.

"Look! There is Ping!" exclaimed Blue Lotus, pulling at her mother's arm and pointing.

The boy's back was turned toward them, but his mother knew at once that it was indeed Ping. And although she did not see his face, she read the longing and the patient acceptance with which he watched the laughing, chattering children coming out of school. For a long minute she watched, and quietly she let the flower of hope fall from her heart to the pavement. Quietly she said to Blue Lotus, "Do not tell Ping that we saw him."

Blue Lotus often spoke without thinking, and now she asked, "Why?"

"Does a child ask her mother why?" said Mrs. Chang, speaking this time so very quietly that Blue Lotus was frightened by the thought of her own undutifulness.

"Please, please forgive me, Mother! I shall be as silent as a stone."

"That is better," said Mrs. Chang, in the same gentle voice. Then she went quickly into the shop with Blue Lotus, out of Ping's sight if he should turn, and took a long time to choose her few needles. When they came out, Ping was gone. As usual, the three met on the steep path, Mrs. Chang and Blue Lotus climbing slowly, Ping running down with his shoeshine box.

The next morning went much as usual, but after they had all eaten a bite of lunch at the market, something very unusual happened. Mrs. Chang bowed to the old woman who sold flowers near them. "May I leave Blue Lotus and the vegetables under your eye, Grandmother?" she asked, using the title of respect. "I wish to take Ping with me today. We will be away for an hour."

"Certainly, certainly," said the old woman. "Blue Lotus and I are good friends."

Ping could not imagine where his mother was taking him, nor why. But he did not ask. She would tell him when she was ready.

In silence they came to the office where the foreign women worked, the doctor and the nurses and the others who asked questions and wrote down answers. Ping looked all about him in wonder, but he hid his feelings. It is not polite to seem surprised by anything. He sat beside his mother on a bench for what seemed a long time, until the doctor came in.

"What may I do for you, Mrs. Chang?" she asked, speaking in Chinese.

Then Mrs. Chang stood up and her words poured out almost like Blue Lotus's, but so low that the lady doctor had to come nearer to hear her.

"You have been very good to me," said Mrs. Chang, "but I have come to tell you that I do not need any more of the medicines, nor to waste your honorable time with healing me. And we can get along without a new apartment, if only you will help my son to go to school. That is more important to us than anything else."

Ping looked at his mother as though he could not believe his ears. How had she guessed? And to think that she would give up getting well and an apartment, too, for his sake! But no! That must not be!

"There is no question of your not going on with your medical care, Mrs. Chang. And as for the apartment, that, too, has been arranged for. But to return to your suggestion. If Ping went to school, how would you get along?"

"My daughter could help me at the market," said Mrs. Chang.

"And I should still carry the water up to our house and shine shoes after school," said Ping, dizzy with hope.

"Then I think everything can be settled," said the doctor. "As you know, Hong Kong is swamped with refugees coming in every day. The city has never been able to keep up with them, in housing or in schools or in anything but the barest necessities such as food. Hong Kong builds as fast as it can, but still, as you know, there are always newer refugees sleeping on the streets and in the arcades. When

it comes to school, however, we at this office are able to do a little, in a few cases in which we become interested. And we will help Ping."

The doctor spoke to one of her assistants. "Have you time to measure Ping? There is a tape measure in the top drawer of my desk." And when the assistant smiled and rose, the doctor turned again to Ping. "Here," she said, "is a young lady who will measure you for your school clothes, and I myself will make arrangements at the school. Come back at this time a week from today."

And that is how Ping's secret became known and his dreams came true. Now, after some months of waiting for the apartment building to be finished, the Changs live in two pleasant rooms, with windows of real glass and running water and a door which locks with a key, and they have a real stove and real beds and a flowering plant on the window-sill. And every day Ping goes to school, wearing a white shirt and dark blue shorts and shoes and socks, with a satchel over his back, and when he comes out, he is laughing and chattering with the other boys, just as he used to long to do. But still he hurries, hurries to get back to his mother and Blue Lotus, who by this time will be home from market. He has his school papers to show them, with the teacher's mark which means "good" and, once in a while, "very good." His mother and Blue Lotus can't read, but they recognize the teacher's marks.

"I am sure the ancestors are pleased with you, my son," his mother says softly as Ping goes out, his shoeshine box over the shoulder which has recently carried the school satchel. He is as proud of one as he is of the other. Is he not Ping, a schoolboy, it is true, but, also and always, the man of the family?

The Four
Little Brothers

THE MOUNTAINS

High, high, high are the mountains of Tibet,
And the mountain winds are cold.
In Lhasa stands the palace of the Dalai Lama,
And its roofs are bright with gold.
Strangers sit in our strong-walled houses,
Strangers crowd down our market street,
And there is strange talk in another language
When strangers meet.

At our high passes the prayer wheels are not turning,
No one adds carved stone to stone,
The sacred images of the gods gleam in deserted temples.
Untended and alone.
High, high, high are the holy mountains,
Blinding-white in their mantles of snow.
They talk with the winds and the skies,
But someday they will notice
What has happened below.

The Four
Little Brothers

In the Tibetan border village of Mangnang, there was great excitement. Word had spread that His Holiness, the Dalai Lama, escaping from the enemies who had invaded the country, would spend the night in Mangnang on his way to India, where he would be safe at last. Already along the trail, great pots of incense had been lighted in honor of his arrival.

The four little brothers, Sonam, Buchung, and Kunchock, with the littlest, Tashi, on Sonam's back, ran out of their house to watch for his coming. Suddenly, they heard the click of ponies' hoofs growing louder along the trail from the high snowy pass above the settlement.

"See!" said Tashi, pointing over Sonam's shoulder. He knew that the others were excited, but did not know exactly why.

Sonam called to his mother, who had remained indoors. "Mother! Mother! His Holiness is here!"

And she, too, ran down the steps from the living quarters above the stable and joined the little boys to watch the fugitives ride slowly into the village. Many of the riders' eyes were red with snow glare and dust storms, and the hard-ridden ponies were stumbling as they walked.

When the watchers saw a young man wearing dark glasses and riding a white horse, everyone seemed to know at once that this was the Dalai Lama. Such an honor had never before come to their village, and although all knew that now it was a very dangerous honor, the people bowed low, with joyful faces, raising their joined hands to their foreheads. Even little Tashi, peering over Sonam's shoulder, tried to raise his fat hands to his forehead, and the young man in black glasses, glancing up, saw him and smiled.

Soon at the edge of the village the attendants put up tents where the travelers would sleep. But that night the rain came, cold and bitter and driving, finding holes in the travel-worn felt and wetting the exhausted occupants.

Next morning there was a murmur through the village: "His Holiness is ill! The Dalai Lama cannot ride this morning!"

Amid the uneasy excitement, a chamberlain appeared at the door of the house where the four little brothers lived. "We are bringing His Holiness here until he is better," said the chamberlain, addressing the mother.

"Oh, this house is not worthy of sheltering His Holiness!" she cried, ashamed of her poverty. "It is so small, so smoke-stained, so poor! He will scorn such a place as this."

"His Holiness must have a good roof over his head while he is ill," said the chamberlain, "and your house seems to be no worse than the others. The Dalai Lama himself asked to be brought to the house of the four little brothers."

After that their mother made no further objection, and the Dalai Lama's cot was carried up the stone steps to the living quarters and set up in the least crowded corner. Soon the Dalai Lama himself was helped up the steps, and thanked the woman and smiled at the four little boys before falling into an exhausted sleep.

"Is he in immediate danger?" the mother asked anxiously, in a low voice.

"Who knows?" said the chamberlain. "Some of our soldiers are behind us, and they will die before the enemy comes near His Holiness. But . . . ," and his tired voice trailed off into silence.

The mother glanced at the young man on the cot. "He is Tibet," she said.

"Yes, he is Tibet," said the chamberlain.

All that day the two watched while the Dalai Lama slept, and the little boys watched, too, and even Tashi understood that he must be very, very quiet.

In the late afternoon the Dalai Lama wakened and ate. He seemed stronger than in the morning and sat cross-legged on his cot, resting his back against the wall. While he ate, he asked the children their names.

"When I was a little older than Tashi and a little younger than Kunchock, I, too, lived on a farm," he told them. "Our mountain was called The Mountain Which Pierces the Sky, and on that mountain lived the guardian deity of our valley. Here, undisturbed, were to be found deer and wild asses, monkeys and leopards, bears and foxes among the flowers and wild plum trees."

"I should like to go to that village!" said Buchung, and then covered his mouth with shame for having spoken when he had not been asked a question.

Next morning, the Dalai Lama was still weak, but he knew that he must go on. Before he left, he gave the mother a ceremonial scarf.

"When you come to India, send this scarf to me, and I will help you and your little sons if I can," he said. Then a look of deep sadness crossed his face. "I am afraid that my presence now brings not a blessing, but a curse. Do not delay."

When the Dalai Lama and his followers were gone, the mother folded the scarf, put on all her dowry of turquoise and coral jewelry, and dressed herself and the children in their newest clothes and boots. Then she made up a packet of food and blankets and strapped these on the best yak and lifted the three littlest children to its back.

"You and I will walk," she told Sonam. "Your father is in the high hills with the fighters. He cannot come with us, but it will be our prayer that later he may join us, and wherever we go we will leave word that we were there, so that if he looks for us he may find us. For the present, we must take care of ourselves. The enemy will follow on the trail of His Holiness, and I think that there will be much killing. If we remain here, the first to die will be those under whose roof His Holiness rested."

Most of the other villagers decided that they, too, had no choice but to follow the Dalai Lama to India.

At first they traveled together in a long strung-out cavalcade, climbing up one snowy, windswept pass and down into the next valley, only to climb again. In the scattered Hindu villages to which they came after crossing the border, they met with a kind welcome, and the people gave them what they could spare.

Days later, as they traveled on out of the Indian hills, the cold mountain air began to grow warmer, and at last, below them, the travelers could see the hot and shimmering plains of India.

The other families from Mangnang decided to stay in the hills. "We can make some kind of living here, but in the plains we should die."

The mother would not remain with them. "Where His Holiness is, is Tibet," she said.

"Have pity on your little sons," a woman begged her.

"Whether they live or die, they will have merit in following His Holiness's footsteps," she answered obstinately, and went on with only the yak and the four little boys for company.

When they reached the steaming heat of the plains, they all suffered, especially the woman. There seemed to be a weight on their heads, and their lungs, accustomed only to the cold, thin air of the mountains, found the lowland air difficult to breathe. Sweat ran down their faces and wet the

backs of their coats, and their thoughts came as
slowly as their bodies moved. The yak suffered with
them, panting and often stopping, its legs spread
as though only so could it keep itself on its feet.

"He's losing his hair, Mother," said Sonam on the
second day, and indeed, the yak's heavy, coarse
hair was coming out by the handful.

"He should go back to the hills," said the woman.

"And may we go back, too?" begged Buchung.

"At least to the last village where we were? The people there were good to us, and it seemed more like home."

His mother wiped the sweat out of her eyes and shook her head. "No," she said. "Where the Dalai Lama goes, we must follow."

Here, where there was trade with Tibet, the woman found a merchant speaking Tibetan, who told her that the Dalai Lama and his followers had left their riding animals and taken a train.

"A train?" she repeated. "What is that?"

"Look and you will see one," said the man.

Just at that moment, something noisy and terrifying came rushing toward them, trailing behind it smoke like the smoke of some enormous torch.

"It is a demon!" whispered the woman, and began to pray, while Tashi, usually so quiet, bawled and tried to scramble off the yak and into his mother's arms.

The man laughed. "It is only a train," he said. "It is not alive. See, it is stopping at the platform. And people are getting in and out of its belly."

"And the Dalai Lama entered into a monster like this?" asked the woman, soothing Tashi.

"Yes, and it carried him off like the wind. If you wish to follow him, you, too, must enter into a train, and do not be afraid of it, in spite of its stamping and shrieking. It will serve you and do you no harm."

"What must be, must be," said the mother. "Be quiet, Tashi. The train will not hurt you. But, sir, what must we do to be able to enter a train?"

"Pay," said the man. "You must pay money before the keepers of the train will let you ride in one."

"I have no money," she said.

"But you have a yak, and I have money," said the merchant, grinning broadly. "I trade in the hills and can use the beast there."

And with that he drove a hard bargain, yet not so hard as he might have, for he was a little touched by the difficulties before them, which he could guess at so much better than they. He also bought most of their blankets at his own figure, but he took the five back to his house, where his wife fed them, and he also gave them food for their journey and, later in the day, took them to the station to see to the buying of their tickets.

"You will not be able to go as far as the Dalai Lama has gone," he warned them. "But at least you can go part of the way."

In spite of the stifling heat, the little boys loved the train.

"We are flying. Yes, we are flying!" they kept saying. "See, Mother, the temples and the great trees! See the carts! Is that a camel? Oh, what wonders!"

And their mother nodded and smiled, but could not speak because of her terror.

They seemed to have gone halfway across the world, when they were told to get down, that their tickets would take them no further. Here in this new place, no one at first could understand what the woman said, but at last she found a man who could speak a little Tibetan.

"The Dalai Lama?" he repeated. "They say he has gone to Mussoorie, and that is far, far from here."

"Then I will sell my jewels," said the woman, "and we will go on by bullock cart."

"I have a cart," said the man, "and I am going toward Mussoorie in a day or two. If you have money, I will take you and your sons, and meantime you may sleep in my courtyard."

He showed them where he lived, and then the mother went to the bazaar with the boys and sat with her Tibetan jewelry spread out on the ground before her. But although many looked, no one offered her more than a handful of coppers for it.

Discouraged and exhausted, she took the boys back to a corner of the courtyard where they had been offered shelter. They were given a little food and, soon after eating, fell into tired sleep. The mother's dreams were bad. A demon was carrying her off—no, it was not she who was being carried off, but the pack under her head, which was being slowly, slowly edged away while a bundle of rags was slipped into its place. Still only half-awake, she seized one corner of her pack and struggled to her knees.

Suddenly, out of the darkness, an unseen hand gave her a violent shove, but she was strong and held on. Now she was shouting for help and stumbling to her feet. She could not see her assailant, but she could hear his heavy breathing as they jerked and tugged at the pack. The boys had been wakened by the noise, and already Sonam was kicking at the thief's ankles and bold Buchung had found a stick and was hitting him. All at once the woman let go and grappled with the man. She was taller and stronger than he, and fearless with desperation, but he, too, now dropped the pack, and she caught his wrist just as he drew a knife from his belt. Twist and turn as he could, the woman still held on, shouting and shouting for help.

It seemed a long time before the man of the
house called from a window, "What's this hubbub
going on?"

"We're being murdered!" shouted the woman.

A light was struck, and the bullock master ran
out of the house with a club. At his approach, the
thief made a final effort and broke free, stooping to
snatch up the pack as he ran, but Sonam had taken
it, and the man escaped, empty-handed.

"Fine doings," said the master of the house when he heard the story. "I see that I must buy the things myself. Last week my wife gave me my first son. I have been thinking of a present for her."

And he bargained. Very little money changed hands, but he agreed to carry the family toward Mussoorie for a certain number of days.

"Surely we shall then be nearly there," said the woman.

The man said nothing. It was not his business to enlighten her.

So, for a few days, the five traveled by cart across the plains of India. The bullocks moved slowly, the cart jounced and creaked, the stinging insects gathered, but with every mile they were a mile nearer Mussoorie. At the beginning of the journey, the wife of the driver had run out with a torn umbrella as a parting gift, so the mother had something to hold between herself and the cruel sun.

All too soon the bullock cart came to its destination, surely sooner than the mother had understood when she made her bargain with the driver, counting the days of travel on her fingers, but the man motioned for them to get out, and that was all they could do.

Yet, like the man who had bought the yak, the

driver, too, was not without pity and took them to his brother-in-law's hut, where they were allowed to sleep in the shed with the cow, while the woman of the place gave them some milk.

Next day they started off on the long road to Mussoorie, the mother carrying Tashi on her back, with the decrepit umbrella still held over her head. Oh, that long road! They followed it for days and weeks and months, through dust and the fierce rains of the rainy season. They saw it bright and terrible with lightning, and forded streams which almost carried the woman off her feet as she crossed, taking one child at a time on her back.

The mother had learned to speak a few words now, and at every stop along the way, to each person who would listen, she repeated her husband's name and, pointing to herself and the children, said, "Mussoorie." She had not much hope that her husband would come. But who knows? Only the gods. So she left a frail track of words across the terrible Indian plains for him to follow, if he came.

When at last, footsore, and thin with fever and half-starved, they reached Mussoorie, they found that the Dalai Lama was no longer there. A woman in the bazaar told them, "He has gone to Dharmsala, in the hills, where the air is cooler. Our heat was not for him, and our government has given him two or three bungalows there. Come, I will take you to some people whose whole business is to help Tibetan refugees."

So the five went on again, this time in a Red Cross truck, driving up and up out of the plains.

The driver was Tibetan and with his own eyes he had more than once seen the Dalai Lama. "I have a little girl the age of one of your children," he said. "She is at Dharmsala, in a nursery in charge of the elder sister of the Dalai Lama. Oh, but she is happy there, eating good food, speaking Tibetan, and following our ways. Sometimes His Holiness comes to see the children. They are under his care."

The long journey was almost over. Once again it seemed that they could breathe in this thinner, cooler air. When the truck drove up to the door of a large bungalow, there were children everywhere, Tibetan children, who stared at them with friendly curiosity. The mother, with the four little boys close to her skirts, knocked at the door, and after some time a tired-looking young woman appeared.

She gave the newcomers a harried glance. "I'm sorry," she said. "We have more children than we can pack into this house. You will have to go someplace else."

"Take them back to the Red Cross office at Mussoorie," she called to the driver. "We can't possibly find room for them here."

The boys stared up at the young woman, speechless. Tashi began to cry. Frowning, the woman waited for them to be gone, and at last the mother started toward the truck, obeying like a sleepwalker. But as she bent to enter the cab, the almost empty pack on her back scraped against the metal of the doorframe.

With renewed hope, she swung around to face the woman, who was still guarding the open door. Clumsy with exhaustion, she took the pack from her shoulders and, opening it, brought out something wrapped in a clean cloth. This one thing she had saved when she sold the yak, sold her turquoise and silver pendants and earrings, sold the coral necklaces and the belt clasp. Carefully she brought out the scarf which the Dalai Lama had given her so long ago in Mangnang.

"His Holiness himself told me to send this to him if we should ever be in India," she whispered.

A change came over the tired face of the young woman. Bowing low, and carrying the scarf in both hands like a relic, she at once led the five to the Dalai Lama's sister, a tall, kind-faced woman.

"Of course," said Tsering Dolma, when she had heard their story. "Until things are straightened out here, you shall sleep in my own room, just as His Holiness once slept in your house. He has told me about it. I am going to his bungalow now and I will take you with me."

As they came into the room where the Dalai Lama was sitting, lost in thought, he looked up, and at sight of the newcomers his face lightened and his eyes smiled.

"Here you all are!" he exclaimed. "Sonam and Buchung and—let me see, yes—Kunchock and Tashi. I have never forgotten you. So you will stay at my sister's nursery? And your mother shall stay with you to help with the care of all the children."

"Will you tell us more stories about what happened when you were a little boy, Your Holiness?" asked bold Buchung.

"Hush! Hush!" murmured his mother.

But the Dalai Lama smiled at Buchung.

"Of course I will tell you stories! Where I was born, the Chinese claimed the province as they now claim all Tibet. Have I told you how the Chinese governor of my province tested some of us little Tibetan boys to see which one of us had been selected to be the new Dalai Lama when the old Dalai Lama

died? The governor wanted a great tribute before he would let the future Dalai Lama go to Lhasa, but he did not know who among the little children had been chosen. So what do you think he did?"

The four little brothers, even Tashi, had been listening intently and now shook their heads.

"He brought out a great box of candies and passed it among us. Some of the little boys were so shy, they would not take any. Some were greedy and took all they could hold in both hands. One little boy took one candy and ate it politely. Then the Chinese governor was certain which of the children was to be the next Dalai Lama."

"And it was you, Your Holiness!" cried Buchung.

The Dalai Lama nodded, smiling. "I hope you will come often to listen to my stories. When I tell them I am happy for they take me back to Tibet and to my own childhood."

The mother bowed low again, and the four little brothers bowed with her.

"Where Your Holiness is, Tibet is," said the woman, and they all looked at the Dalai Lama, their thin faces blazing with the happiness of people who have at last come to the end of a long, hard quest.

The Decision

JOLANDA'S SONG

Katie,
My doll, Katie,
Is very, very clever,
And she's very, very sweet.

But she's too young to remember
The house we used to live in,
With its little sunny windows
Looking on the street.

And she's too young to remember
The cheerful church bells ringing,
And the distant sound of singing
From the church, so gray and old.

I can't remember, either—
I'm rather young like Katie—
But I listen very carefully
To everything I'm told.

The Decision

Jolanda woke up suddenly with the old feeling of terror, but she had learned not to cry out and disturb the others. A rat had just run across the foot of her cot. In the darkness, Jolanda's first move was to reach for Katie, her one-eyed doll and greatest comfort. Then she heard low voices. The lamp was not burning, but the grown-ups were sitting by the stove at the end of the small room, talking in low voices. It was her father's voice she heard first, with its half-hidden note of anger.

"Our papers were on the table before him. He was studying them as I came in and kept me standing. At last he looked up. 'Yes,' he said, 'Australia will take you as soon as you can get ready. All but your son, Andreas. The T.B. rules him out.'

" 'But, sir,' I said, 'his illness has been cured. The doctor here noticed it early.' 'That may be as may be,' he said. 'Australia isn't taking him or anyone else with weak lungs.' Nothing I could say would move him."

There was the sound of a woman crying in the darkness.

"Stop that sniveling!" exclaimed the father. "I have told you now, while the children are asleep, so that each of you may give your advice. Be silent until you have thought well, and then speak. But we've had enough of tears."

The grandmother was the first to speak.

"What you say, my son, brings me a certain happiness. In these long years since we escaped from Hungary, I have been only a burden to you all."

"No, no," said the man, "never that."

"You are kind," went on the old woman. Jolanda was surprised to hear anyone call her father kind, but sometimes he was. "Still, the wonderful future in Australia is not for me. I will stay here and cook for Andreas and mend his clothes. He will not be alone. There will be someone of his own blood beside him, and when he marries"—she gave a little laugh—"I will dance at his wedding!"

"You are a good woman, Mother," said her son somberly. "I will remember what you have said."

After a while, Jolanda's mother spoke in a voice that still sounded tearful. "Can't we go back?" she

begged. "Can't we go back to our own village? Some of the families are going back! The government has promised a pardon to everyone who left the country. Our own house! Our own church again! Our friends about us! We cannot even speak the language of the Australians! Dear husband, let us go back."

"And what of freedom?" the father asked harshly. "But you both have told me what is in your hearts. Do not speak of it again, even to one another. It is time we were in bed."

Jolanda lay very still, holding tight to Katie. What did it all mean? Would she and Katie go to Australia and see the kangaroos and koala bears? Some of the other children were going there, but poor Andreas! Still, if Grandmother stayed with him, it might not be so bad. The two of them, perhaps, would have all three rooms for themselves. The rooms were only like big packing boxes, knocked quickly together a long time ago during the war and then made use of by the Austrians to house the refugee Hungarians as they poured into their country. Jolanda had been born at the camp. It was home to her, but even she knew it was a sad home.

She listened to all the stories of their real home, the Hungarian one, and of the flowers there and the market held once a week in the square and the dancing! Sometimes she thought she had been there herself, she loved it so. But, no, she and her older sister and second brother and Katie, the doll, were camp children. Only Andreas had been born in Hungary.

At breakfast at the crowded table, with some of the family sitting on the foot of the cots and Andreas on an old trunk, there was less talk than usual. The father never said a word. If any of the children spoke to him, he either grunted or didn't appear to hear. The mother's eyes were red from crying. Only the old grandmother acted as if nothing were wrong. Her cheerful, thin voice went on as usual, speaking of the neighbors, asking about school.

But the children were all quiet. Only Jolanda knew anything, and she hadn't spoken of what she knew.

"Be silent!" her father had said, and her father was a man whom everyone obeyed. The other children were like sea birds who feel a storm in the air. What it might be, they didn't know, but they were uneasy.

Andreas, in particular, felt trouble coming. Why did the grown-ups glance at him so often when they thought he was not looking? He felt his mother's tearful eyes watching him, his father's dark, fierce glance brooding on him. Even little Jolanda kept looking at him as if he had grown two noses. He was glad when it was time to go to school and he and Ivan, his younger brother, and the girls could get out of the house, until the storm had had time to blow over.

But the storm did not blow over. For three days the father brooded, the mother wept silent tears, and the grandmother stirred about, humming cheerfully. For three days Jolanda whispered to Katie, and Katie, as usual, stared at nothing from her one blue eye.

But at supper at the end of the third day, the father spoke, just after the soup had been served, and everyone at the table, even the grandmother, stopped eating to hear him.

"There has been a question as to what we are to do, and I have wrestled with it long and hard," he said. "We might go to Australia to begin a new life. But because Andreas has once been ill, he could not go, and your grandmother has offered, in that case, to stay with him. We might return to Hungary, humble ourselves, and speak or be silent as our dictators directed. Or we might stay here, at Linz, in Austria. Soon there will be new, decent apartments to take the place of these refugee dumps. Three of you children were born here and speak German better than Hungarian. I myself have work most days in the week. It is easy to stay where one is, to continue on the accustomed road. Many times I have asked myself, in agony, if that is why I have come to the decision that we should stay here. Who knows? But, I think, God has given us one another, and it cannot be God's will that we should choose to be separated. As for returning to a life in Hungary, where we should never be free, I do not know what God wills. But *I* do not will it."

The father looked sternly about the table.

"What do you say? Are you all dumb?" he demanded.

Jolanda was the first to move. She was the youngest and had special privileges. Now she jumped up, still holding Katie in one arm and throwing the other about her father's neck, pressed Katie's nose hard into his cheek.

"I'm so glad we're staying," Jolanda said. "I love all my class in school and the teacher."

"Well, well," said her father, patting her shoulder and Katie's, too, and pushing them away, gently enough.

It was Andreas' turn now. "Thank you, sir. I am

very grateful," Andreas said, standing straight and thin.

Suddenly the father's eyes softened.

"You are a good son," he said. "I could not leave you behind. Nor your grandmother, either."

After that, everyone spoke up at once, and the father laughed his short, barking laugh. "You are like a flock of geese. I cannot hear what you say. But I see from your faces that you are glad. Perhaps you, Marya," he added, "would have preferred something else, but a woman is happy where her husband is. Come, our porridge is getting cold. We must not waste good food."

Jolanda went back to her seat and gave Katie an imaginary bite of porridge. Yes, now that Father had made his hard decision, the sun was shining again. Even Mother looked more cheerful. She would carry the village in her heart and lovingly describe it to the children. It was a golden keepsake that no one could take from her. But, as always, her husband had said a true word. Where her family was, was home for her.

"Off to school with you, longlegs!" shouted the grandmother, shaking her skirts as if she were shooing a flock of chickens, and off the children ran, laughing.

The father lighted his pipe, but before going to work, he touched his wife's shoulder as he went out.

"Don't think I don't understand you," the touch said. "Perhaps it is hardest for you. But we will make a good new life together."

When he had gone, the grandmother bustled about. "That child!" she pretended to scold. "She never remembers to put Katie away. Yet, after all, there's no place to put things in these barracks. By next year, the new brick apartments the U.N. is building will be finished and this place will be burned down, and good riddance! Running water, they say we shall have, and larger windows and even electric lights. We shall live like royalty next year, Marya. You are still young, and there is a good future ahead of you."

"But when my time comes to die, I shall not lie in the graveyard in the shadow of our church," said the mother, and she put her arms about the old woman and cried her last tears on her shoulder.

Then she sat up and patted her hair in place. "Come," she said cheerfully. "This is washday, and we have much to do. Katie's dress, too, needs washing. I wonder if there is not someone who could put that lost eye back in place? It's still inside her head."

"A good idea," said the grandmother. "Do you know what the other children say?

> " 'One-eyed Katie
> Went to Haiti,
> And that's what became
> Of one-eyed Katie!' "

The mother laughed, such a pretty laugh.

"We'll have Katie fixed somehow!" she said.

Suddenly, now that she knew at last, after so many years of uncertainty, where they were going to be, she could begin to make plans again for the future.

"Yes," she repeated, "somehow we must get Katie fixed and surprise Jolanda."

The Cattle

LAMENT

Aie! the cattle! the beautiful cattle!
Each one walks like a chief.
A man's herd is his reason for boasting,
And they are his comfort in grief.
They wander and graze, wide-horned and gentle,
Clean-limbed, slow-stepping, great-eyed—
His cattle are a man's proof of manhood:
They are his wealth, and their beauty his pride.

But now we have fled from our village
And left our cattle behind,
We fled for our lives with what little we could carry,
We fled, huddled and blind.
South, south, south, we poured, running in terror,
And left our village and our garden plots and our stream,
All, all behind, and now we live among strangers
Like people who move in the shadows of a dream.

I once had twelve head of cattle.
Their horns were as long as a sword.
The best was named He-Who-Fears-Nothing,
And the others all knew him as lord.
What am I now without my herd beside me?
And my son, the child of a cattleless man?
We are without honor or joy in a strange country.
We should have died.
But we ran.

The Cattle

Now, for Pierre the two most important people in the world were his father and Mr. Fischer. His father was a Watusi, tall, thin, with cavernous eyes. Wrapped in a white robe, he was like someone already dead. He looked out on the world about him, the world of exile, with complete indifference.

If his wife or Pierre or anyone else told him something or asked him a question, he had only one answer. "What does it matter?" And even his voice seemed to come from someplace far off.

He was a Watusi, and Pierre knew very well what that meant. It meant the honor of being owner of a herd of great, long-horned cattle, which he would take to graze, defending them to the death from lions or any other danger. His herd was a Watusi's pride. Ages ago the tribe had come from the north. No one knew just from where they had come, tall men, black, with thin noses and thin lips, following their herds as they grazed, carrying long spears in their hands. The people in Rwanda had been awed by them, by their height, by their hawk-like courage, above all by their cattle, and they had accepted them as their overlords. Each Watusi was a noble. To follow his herd and to fight were his occupations. The other tribes did the rest.

Pierre had been brought up to this life. So it had been, so it would always be. But there was turmoil in Africa, and the subject tribes, who were far greater in number, rose against the Watusi and killed many of them and their households. Pierre's father was among those who escaped to Burundi, over the border. He kept on walking until he reached Tanzania. To save his family, he had left his cattle behind, and now his only wish was to die.

For many months it seemed that he would get his wish. In Tanzania he and the other Watusi like him had been given a village named Muyenzi in which to live. Their crops failed for lack of rain or irrigation. Food was scarce. The women did what they could, but the men sat and looked into the distance.

Then they were offered beautiful land in the highlands, green and fed by springs.

"We will stay here," said Pierre's father. "Here we will die almost in sight of our old homes. This is better for us than the finest land far from our birthplace."

The other thin black chiefs nodded their heads. "This Muyenzi is not a good place to live in, but it will do very well to die in."

The women listened, their children in their arms. They themselves did not mind starving very much, but they wished the children to live.

When they were alone, Pierre's mother said to his father, "But Pierre and little Celeste?" Celeste was Pierre's younger sister.

Pierre's father frowned. His heart pained him at her words.

"It is better for them, too," he said quietly. He always spoke quietly, but Pierre's mother said nothing more.

It was at this time, when the chiefs would not move to better land, that the Tanzanian government asked for help from the United Nations.

One day Pierre ran into his father's house. "A strange man has come, a white man. He is to see to affairs in the village. He is called Mr. Fischer. He is not tall, but he is strong and has a red face and yellow hair. He speaks in our language, but he makes

funny mistakes. It is hard to keep from laughing."

Pierre's mother was interested, but his father said in his faraway voice, "What is he to me?"

"He has brought food in a truck and tomorrow will give it out to each family. We are each to have ten acres of our own, to plant gardens, and he has brought seeds."

"Has he brought rain?" asked Pierre's father contemptuously, and wrapped his head in his robe and thought of other things.

But Pierre's mother listened. She longed for her children to live. She was almost as tall and thin and beautiful as her husband, but she was only a woman. She had never herded the great long-horned cattle. She had only borne children, and she wanted them to live.

Every day Pierre came back with new tales of what Mr. Fischer was doing.

"Great machines have come now and other white men. They are digging wells for drinking water. Listen, Father, you can hear the loud talk of the machines as they dig. Mr. Fischer says the water of the river is not good to drink."

"It sufficed," said the father. And he refused to go to see how the wells were being dug, though all the children were there and some of the women and a few of the men.

Later Pierre had more to report. "Mr. Fischer is making ponds from the overflow from the wells, and he will stock them with fish for food. He wants me to help with the digging."

"Let him dig in the mud, like a pig," spat out Pierre's father. "Next these white men will raise grasshoppers!" And he would not go to see these marvels.

When the sawmill was set up, he closed his ears to the sound of the saw at work. He did not wish to hear that some of his friends were at work there, making things that the village needed.

Pierre loved the new forge, where tools and spears could be mended, but his father would not go with him to see it.

There was a small hospital now, and Pierre liked the excitement of watching people brought into it to be cured. There was no end to the things Mr. Fischer thought up for the village to do. He had logs laid across a swamp to a place where the soil was damp and good, and there some of the men under his direction were raising corn, peas, cabbage, peanuts, soya, white potatoes, sugarcane and rice.

"Beans and sweet potatoes are good enough for Watusi," said Pierre's father. "Let Mr. Fischer swallow his own trash."

But Pierre and Celeste went to their mother's brother's house and tasted these new things, for their uncle had at last become interested in Mr. Fischer and what he was doing.

"With the irrigation from the fishponds, our crops are safe, even without rain," their uncle said. "Mr. Fischer declares that though Muyenzi may never be home to us who are grown, it may someday be home to you children, and we must make it a good home."

Pierre repeated this to his father, and for once his father answered seriously.

"It is true," he said. "A young plant may be put in new earth and thrive. But an old plant withers away. I have buried my heart in Rwanda. It is for you to become part of this new place, if it must be so."

Pierre looked at him with gratitude. To him his father was like the night, dark and wise and mysterious. Mr. Fischer was like the day, always doing something, making plans, arguing, laughing, scolding.

No one was hungry now. There was laughter in Muyenzi. The children followed Mr. Fischer in a chattering crowd to see what he would do next. One day he said, "We are going to have a school to keep you out of my way." And he laughed, and the children laughed.

"A school for boys," said Pierre proudly.

"For boys and girls," said Mr. Fischer. "Celeste is just as bright as you are, Pierre. She shall go to school, too."

Pierre's mother was excited when the children brought this news.

"May I go to the sewing class and make new clothes out of burlap bags for the children, so that they won't go to school in rags?" she asked her husband when they were alone together.

"It is all one to me whether you go or stay," said Pierre's father, but that evening he stalked through the village on his long legs with the strange dignity of a tall stork.

He said nothing when he came back, either good or bad. Part of Pierre was with him, brooding and sad. But part of Pierre was with Mr. Fischer, with his red face and his laughter, getting things done.

"Was it well with the village, Father?" he ventured to ask.

But his father seemed not to hear him.

All the children followed Mr. Fischer, but perhaps Pierre was with him more often than any of the others.

"Why will your father take no interest in what

is going on?" Mr. Fischer asked him one day.

"He longs for the cattle," said Pierre. "A Watusi's life is in his herd."

"Ah," said Mr. Fischer thoughtfully.

One morning, a month or two later, Pierre, after he had eaten, ran out into the village to see what was happening. There was always something happening nowadays. He could never guess what it would be next. The school was being built, but it was not finished, and the children still trailed Mr. Fischer, their surest amusement and their best teacher.

But this morning, the new thing was so wonderful that Pierre's heart stopped beating and then began to race so fast that his whole body was shaken. He was not his father's son for nothing.

There at the edge of the square stood six trucks, so thickly surrounded by people that at first he could scarcely see what was in them. But even before he saw, he knew. He knew by every sense, by faint sounds, by smell, by the excitement in the air. And then he saw them. The men were unloading gentle, great-horned Watusi cattle from the trucks.

He fought his way through the crowd to Mr. Fischer. "Mr. Fischer?" he panted.

"Yes," said Mr. Fischer. "This is the beginning. Tell your father that each head of a family is to have two. And when he has earned them by his work, there will be more."

Running as fast as his own racing heart, Pierre broke away from the crowd and hurried toward his father's house. Without manners, he cried, "Father! Father! The Watusi cattle have come! Two for every man!"

His father sprang to his feet. He was not ashamed to run. This was what he had craved, what he had believed his eyes would never see again, except in dreams.

He stood beside Mr. Fischer. He laughed like a child. "They have come," he said, over and over, the tears running down his cheeks.

"They have come," said Mr. Fischer. "And more are coming. Now the heads of the families will draw these by lot. Later there will be more for those who will work for them."

Pierre's father's gaunt face was lighted with joy.

"I will work, and all my household with me," he said, and his voice was like a song.

To Pierre watching, standing on one foot, peace had come at last. His night and day were one. His sun and moon shone with a single light. The two halves of his world had been joined, and all was well at last.

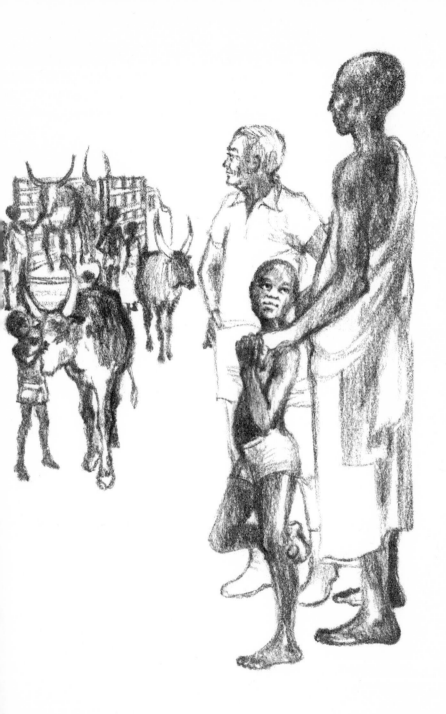

The House
of the Lion

THE LION'S GIFT

He was a very good lion,
(The broken one by the spring.)
At once we liked one another
And he gave us everything:
Quiet, and his own house,
And lucky beads on a string.

He was a very good lion,
And my grandmother was wise.
She didn't listen to what people said,
She looked with her own two eyes,
And she saw that he had given us a palace
And that all the rest was lies.

We lived in the House of the Lion,
We lived without hunger or fear
Until peace brought us back to our village
Where I'm happy—but somehow here
The stars aren't so bright in the evening sky,
And the sun doesn't seem so near.

The House
of the Lion

Leila was very young when she fled with her mother from Algeria into Morocco, where they would be safe from the fighting that was going on all over their country. She was her father's especial pet, his little lamb. On that last visit, when he came home from the war to tell them that they must go, he looked at Leila with troubled eyes. But when he talked to her mother, he sounded cheerful enough.

"Fortunately, we live near the border, so you will not have far to travel, and we have the two donkeys," he told her. "You must load them with tent, food and something to wear when winter comes. Perhaps your mother and sister will go with you. Their Ahmed is a big boy. He will be a help. If you stay here, you all are likely to be killed. But do not cry. Our separation will not be for long. We shall meet at the end of the war, and then our country will be free at last."

Leila's mother did not cry.

"We will be all right," she said. "Never forget us. You live in our hearts."

When Leila's father was gone, her mother hurried to the nearby house where Leila's aunt and grandmother lived with her cousin Ahmed, who was quite a big boy, and little Zohra, who was younger than Leila. Leila's uncle was fighting far off to the east and could not get back to his family to tell them what to do, but they decided to go with Leila and her mother while there was still time to get away. They had one donkey, which they took with them, and they all set out at night under the stars, traveling westward through rough country. When Leila and Zohra grew tired, they took turns riding one of the loaded donkeys, and toward dawn Ahmed carried Zohra on his back. Now and then they rested for a little, while the donkeys grazed. Then they went on again, sometimes following a road and sometimes traveling over wide empty spaces, overgrown with alfa grass.

When the sun rose, they stopped and lighted a very small fire and made breakfast, and while they were eating, a shepherd came up to them, which frightened them, but he greeted them with kindness.

Everyone waited for Ahmed to return the greeting, but to their surprise, it was the grandmother who spoke.

"What country is this?" she asked, covering her face with her veil. She had traveled all night, almost without speaking, saving her strength for walking. But now she spoke.

"This is Morocco," said the man. He was too polite to ask where they came from, but the grandmother had more questions.

"Is there any village ahead?" she asked.

"Yes," said the man. "In two hours' walking, you will come to my village. Good people live there, who remember their duty to wayfarers, many as these have become. None of us has much food left, but the strangers from faraway have established a station. Once a month they give out food for all, so much for each person; and to any children who come to them, every day they give also a cup of milk and a slice of bread. They have doctors and nurses to care for the sick, and they have teachers for the young children."

"You are sure that there is no poison in the food?" asked the grandmother sharply.

"No, there is no poison. My household eats of it daily. We gave all we had to those of you who came first. Now we, too, must take what the strangers give."

"May they be rewarded, then," said the grandmother. "But it is very strange."

"Yes," agreed the shepherd, "it is strange. But some of our own people from the cities are with them. They stand shoulder to shoulder."

"It is a new thing under the sun," said the grandmother. "Let us go on, then, and see these wonders for ourselves."

At first Leila and her relatives lived in their tent. There were other Algerians living in tents and in *gourbis*—huts built with mud and covered with leaves. They all got their water from a spring, which poured out strongly from between the roots of a tree. That first day, Leila's mother and aunt went for water, while the two little girls brought small tins to fill. It was a cool, shady place under the great tree and everyone was tired. Like all Arabs, Leila's mother and aunt loved the sound of a running stream, and so they sat for a little while to rest and enjoy the quiet. Far off below them, beyond the plain, they could see the flash of the sea.

While they sat and talked, the little girls played, and suddenly Leila discovered something in the underbrush.

"Look! Mother!" she cried. "A lion! A lion!"

"Do not be foolish," said her mother. "There are no lions here."

"But truly it is a lion," said Leila.

Her mother got up and went to look. "Truly it is a lion!" she exclaimed to Leila's aunt, laughing a little. "Come and see."

"This is the work of the Romans," said Leila's aunt. "Have I not seen it in the museum in the city of Algiers? Look now, once the water came through the lion's open mouth, but the head has fallen and been broken on the stones. It is better so. I want nothing to do with lions, real ones or marble ones, either."

But Leila liked her stone lion head with its round open mouth and its broken ears.

"Poor lion," she said, and later she talked about it to some of the village children, who came out of their walled village to play with the refugee children.

"That is nothing," said one little boy. "There is a House of the Lion, too, over there in the little valley above the spring. We none of us go near it, because if anyone sleeps in it, the ghost of a lion comes at night and carries him off. My grandfather once walked near the place at dusk and heard something move in the bushes. It was the lion, and if he had not run away, it would have carried him off, too."

Leila, round-eyed, repeated the tale to her family.

"I will go and see this House of the Lion with my own eyes," said her grandmother. "Ahmed, you will come with me."

Ahmed did not want to go with her, but he was not yet a man, and he had to obey his grandmother.

They came back out of breath, but the old woman, at least, was very pleased. "It will be a fine place for us, as I guessed," she said. "It has walls, sometimes five feet high, sometimes seven or eight feet, and door spaces and window spaces. We can have the big room, and the animals will have one of the small ones, and we will stretch our tent cloths across a corner to make a roof."

"But what about the lion?" Leila's aunt asked Ahmed uneasily.

"How can I tell?" said Ahmed, speaking methodically, as was his way. "Someone has partly cleared the old floor, which is made of little pieces of colored stone fitted cleverly together. Around the border there is a pattern of vines, and in it are a quail and a rabbit, harmless enough things. But in the next twist of the vine there stands a lion, roaring, with his mane over his shoulders and his tail stretched out as if ready to charge. Whoever was clearing the floor stopped when he saw the lion, and I myself do not like it, nor think we should go near it."

"Nonsense!" said the grandmother. "It is only a picture, such as we see in the newspapers, and a very good picture. We shall be far more comfortable there than in this crowded tent. Come, it is not late. We have time to move before dark."

Who was there to oppose such a brave, determined old grandmother? Living in their own village, where the men decided everything, no one had dreamed that she was like this, brave as a soldier and determined as a mule. The little girls and their mothers whimpered and protested, Ahmed muttered and scowled, but they had their supper that evening in their new quarters in the House of the Lion, while that night all their acquaintances in the refugee settlement wakened now and then to listen for their screams.

But there were no screams. After their hard night and day, the grandmother scolded them all into sleep and then sat, awake, to guard them, but as she had guessed, there was nothing to guard them from. Morning came, and all was well. Now the ruins of the old villa seemed to belong to them, airy, light and convenient. At night, their little donkeys were safely penned beside them. The thicket near the ruin furnished their firewood. The spring was only a little below them, so that the water carriers had an easy climb coming back with their heavy cans.

"Ah, it is good," said the grandmother, looking about her. "I have always wished to live in a palace, and here I am. But now it is time for Ahmed and the little girls to go down to the Center and bring back food, and they must drink the milk which is given them without fear."

"I shall go with them," said Leila's aunt.

"No," said Leila's grandmother. "There is much still to do to put this house to rights. You are needed here. They will go down with the other children." The old woman looked like an old hawk. No one dared to disobey her.

So down to the valley the three children went together, and they found all the wonders of which they had been told by the shepherd. Ladies in white gave them cups brimming with sweet milk, and with it they were given bread.

Then they were asked whether they would like to go to school. Leila and Zohra sat down on the ground with fifty or more other little girls, like a covey of quail settling, and the teacher began by having them all recite together a verse from the Koran.

The little boys sat in another place, and because Ahmed was the biggest boy, the teacher called on him to write his name on a homemade blackboard leaning against a tree. Ahmed was proud to show how well he knew how to write. He had been to school in Algeria, but, of course, no one expected the girls to go to school.

When Leila's mother and aunt heard that Leila and Zohra had a teacher, too, Leila's mother laughed, but Zohra's mother was angry. "It is not suitable!" she cried. "She will never get a husband with such foolishness!"

But the old grandmother looked up fiercely from the pot where she was cooking dinner. "Foolishness, indeed," she told her daughter, "but the foolishness is yours! Suppose she should marry a shopkeeper? Would he not be glad to have a wife who could keep the accounts? Or a farmer? She could write down his profits from year to year. Or even read to him from the newspaper. Here, tend to the cooking while I clean the floor a little."

Speaking of newspapers made the grandmother think of the pictures on their floor. Already she had uncovered a hound baying at the lion, a wild boar and half a horse, but here some of the stones were worn away. Now, with Ahmed's help, she found in a corner of the room a mosaic cat lying as if asleep.

"It is better to have a palace pavement than mud and broken pottery underfoot," she said, very pleased. "See what I have found, too! These blue beads must have been here since the ancient days. Whose necklace was it, I wonder, and when was it broken?" And she gave each little girl a bit of string so that she might wear about her neck an ancient blue bead as a lucky charm.

These were happy days for the children, and the grandmother was happy, too, in the ruins which she called her palace, but Leila's and Zohra's mothers had heavy hearts, not knowing whether their husbands were alive or dead. Month followed month, and no news of them came, and the war went on and on.

Every day the children walked to the Center to have their milk and bread and to go to school. Every

month provisions were given to each family. Ahmed
and the little girls carried home their share. When
it grew cold, each person was given a blanket,
and there were clothes and coats and shoes distrib-
uted. Where did all these things come from? From
almost every country in the world. Ship after ship
after ship came to the ports, laden with cargo, trucks
roared up long dusty or muddy roads, volunteers un-
loaded heavy bundles and parceled them out to the
hands that waited for them. Never did the magic line
break, by which three hundred thousand people
were preserved in the wilderness.

Meantime Leila's grandmother had dug a garden
and planted seeds, given to her by the people in the
village. And when a woman there was taken ill,
she took care of her, and the granddaughters found
her holding the woman's baby as if it had been her
own. Her hands brought comfort to whatever they
touched. When she found among the refugees an
old, lame Algerian man without kin, she brought
him back to the House of the Lion and added him
to the household. And the children loved him and
called him Grandfather Saïd. At night, after the
meal had been eaten, Grandfather Saïd often told
stories, usually about Mohammed, the prophet of
God.

"Once," he said, "Mohammed, the prophet of God, was sitting on the ground, when a little cat came and laid itself down on his robe and went to sleep beside him. Suddenly the hour for prayer was called, but Mohammed, the prophet of God, would not waken the little cat from its sleep. Instead, he cut a piece from his robe so that he might kneel and say his prayers while the little cat slept, undisturbed."

"Like your little cat on the floor, Grandmother," said Leila, and the grandmother glanced at the mosaic cat and smiled.

One evening Grandfather Saïd asked, "Did you know that Mohammed, the prophet of God, was once a refugee, just as we are? It was before he had many followers, and the people of Mecca became enraged against him because of his teachings and intended to kill him. But Mohammed, the prophet of God, learned of their evil intentions and escaped out of the town. When he was so tired he could go no farther he came to a little cave, and squeezed himself into it, but soon afterward his enemies reached the spot, close at his heels. They saw the cave, and one said, 'He might be in there,' but another said, 'No, it is not possible. See, a spider has spun her web across the entrance.' And so they went on, and by a spider, Mohammed, the prophet of

God, was saved. Never despise anything because it is weak or small, for a spider saved the prophet of God."

Spring came, and now the children found the hills covered with wild flowers. Still the ships never stopped coming into the ports, the trucks never stopped rolling along through the mud, the volunteer workers never stopped unloading the heavy parcels, the teachers never stopped teaching, the doctors and nurses never stopped healing, so that when the news came that there was peace at last in Algeria, the refugees were alive and well to make their return trip. And for Leila's mother and aunt, the best news was that their husbands were alive, too.

"And we will take Grandfather Saïd home with us, for he has no home of his own," said the grandmother.

"But who knows if that will please our husbands?" asked Leila's mother and aunt.

"It pleases me," said the grandmother. "And he shall ride on the strongest of the donkeys."

So once more they started out on a journey, but this time they were filled with hope and happiness. In the lead, Ahmed walked, smiling, and Leila's mother came next, in her flowered dress, and old Grandfather Saïd rode, seated back of the bundles on one donkey, with Leila on the back of another, while her aunt drove the third donkey, with Zohra asleep in one of the panniers.

Right in the middle walked the grandmother, carrying a little load of sticks on her back for the evening fire. She was tired, but she did not ask to ride. She had left behind her beloved palace, the House of the Lion, and when she returned to a dwelling which had a master, she would not speak her mind any more, but would sit in silence over her work.

But the grandmother was satisfied. She had kept them all together, her family, and watched them blossom like the spring flowers. She had saved old Grandfather Saïd. The donkeys were here, and the tent cloths were here, and the baskets. Everything was safe. And best of all, they were well and on their way home at last.

FLIGHT

You who were once a baby
And among strangers born
In a stable with a shabby ass
And an ox with a broken horn,
Who, when the soldiers sought you,
Escaped away in the night,
All hidden in your mother's cloak
On the long road of flight,

Look down on us in pity
Who now must stand alone,
Leaving familiar faces,
And all things we have known:
Our kin, our friends, our houses,
Even the flowers and trees—
You who were of our number,
Pity small refugees!

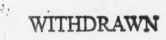